What Kyle Can Do

By Conni Branscom
and Brooke Luckadoo Hicks

Illustrated by Marcin Piwowarski

ISBN: 978-1-943258-27-7

Library of Congress: 2016956964

Editing: Amy Ashby

Published by Warren Publishing, Inc.
Charlotte, NC
www.warrenpublishing.net
Printed in the United States

Thank you to our family, friends and community for all of your support.

Thank you Brooke for your hard work and continued dedication
to advocate for children with special needs.

A special thank you to Amy B for being Kyle's biggest cheerleader.

For more on Kyle's journey
please visit www.kyleskornerinc.org

My name is Mya and I am seven years old. I have a very big family. I have two brothers and one sister. My sister, Aidyn, is three years old. My brother, Kyle, is four years old and I have a new baby brother, Luke. I love spending time with my family and I love being a big sister.

Before Kyle was born, I was so excited to be a big sister. I was happy because I thought me and my new baby brother would be able to do everything together.

When Kyle was born, I was so excited. My mom and dad were happy too, but they told me that Kyle had something called Down syndrome. I was a little sad because I thought this meant that Kyle would not be able to play with me, but I was wrong.

My parents told me that Down syndrome is a genetic disorder that some babies are born with. Babies who are born with Down syndrome have an extra chromosome. Chromosomes are things that make all of us who we are.

My mom and dad explained to me that Kyle and I could still play together, it would just take Kyle longer to learn things because he has Down syndrome. They also told me that Kyle might look different.

Kyle looks different than me and Aidyn and some of the other kids I see. His eyes and mouth are different than most kids because he has Down syndrome. Kyle also has to wear braces on his legs to help him walk better.

Aidyn is younger than Kyle, but she is still able to talk more and do more activities than Kyle is able to do. At first, I did not understand, but now I know that Kyle can do everything he wants to, it will just take some extra time.

Many people think that my family is different because I have a brother with Down syndrome. I think Kyle makes my family special. We enjoy spending time with him and learning from him.

Even though Kyle has Down syndrome, he can still do many exciting things.

He can play on the playground.

He can make silly faces.

He can play in the sand.

He can hold his baby brother.

He can swing.

He can make other people happy. He can also make himself happy!

He can go to school.

He can play in the pool.

He can play baseball.

Although Kyle has Down syndrome, he is still a fun, loving, and playful boy. He makes our family special and makes people smile every day.

Kyle can do so many great things and will continue to do great things throughout his entire life!

CPSIA information can be obtained
at www.ICGtesting.com
Printed in the USA
LVRC02n0032200117
521606LV00005BA/13